Aurora

Sleeping Beauty

GW00726773

PaRragon

Bath · New York · Singapore · Hong Kong · Cologne · Delhi
Melbourne · Amsterdam · Johannesburg · Shenzhen

This edition published by Parragon in 2012
Parragon
Chartist House
15-17 Trim Street
Bath, BA1 1HA, UK
www.parragon.com

ISBN 978-1-4454-6528-9

Printed in China

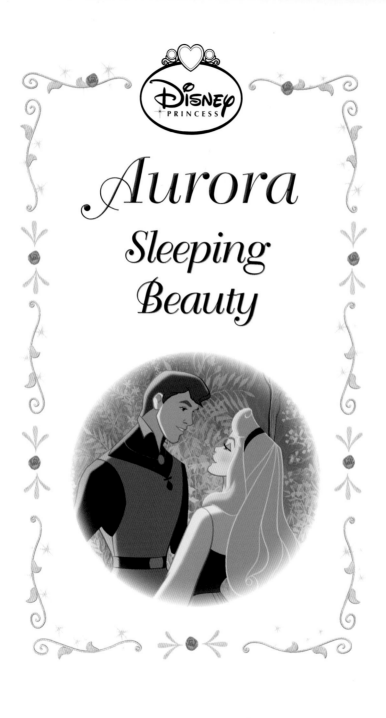

Aurora

Sleeping Beauty

Chapter One

A long time ago, in a faraway land, there was a king and a Queen who longed for a child. One day, their wish was granted. The Queen gave birth to a beautiful daughter, whom they named Aurora, after the dawn. The baby Princess Aurora filled their lives with sunshine, and King Stefan declared there would be a great party to celebrate her birth.

There were knights, lords and ladies,

farmers and peasants, all coming together to mark this special day. Hundreds of fireworks were seen in the sky, there were colourful streamers lining all the streets and trumpets playing joyful music could be heard for miles around the castle. "Long live the Princess Aurora!" everyone cried as they marched and danced through the town.

A very good friend of the king and Queen's, King Hubert, arrived from a

neighbouring kingdom, and with him he brought his young son, Prince Phillip. Eager to unite the two kingdoms, Aurora's father, King Stefan, announced that Prince Phillip and Princess Aurora were betrothed to each other and would marry on Aurora's sixteenth birthday. Just as everyone was toasting this happy news, there was a loud fanfare that rang through the great hall of the castle.

"Their royal excellencies," a court guard announced, "the three good fairies!"

There was a shimmer of light that cascaded down from a window in the hall as, one by one, Flora, Fauna and Merryweather flew down to greet the baby princess.

"Congratulations, your Majesties!" the three fairies said at once.

"We would each like to offer the Princess Aurora one gift each, no more, no less," said

Flora as she floated over to the baby.

"Lovely princess," Flora continued, "my gift to you is the gift of beauty." The fairy waved her wand over the sleeping princess and dozens of glittering sparks drifted gently downwards. Flora stepped back and Fauna flitted over to the baby.

"Dearest princess," said Fauna, "my gift, shall be the gift of song." She raised her wand and little swirls appeared in the air and

surrounded Princess Aurora's crib.

Merryweather, the last of the fairies to present her gift, flew happily to the princess and raised her wand. But before she could utter a word, a great draught swept through the hall.

Suddenly there was the loud CRACK! of a thunderbolt, a flash of green fire and a tall, dark, sinister figure appeared in the middle of the hall.

"Maleficent!" whispered Flora, in dismay.

Maleficent was an evil fairy, who lived with her monstrous guards and her pet raven in her castle on the Forbidden Mountain. She was feared by the whole kingdom.

"What does she want here?" asked Merryweather. The three good fairies looked at each other in alarm. What could Maleficent be planning?

Maleficent cast her cold eyes over the king, the Queen and the fairies. "Your Majesties," she said, bowing slightly. Her eyes fell on the princess lying in her crib.

"M-Maleficent!" stammered the Queen nervously. "What a surprise!"

"Please allow me to offer my congratulations on the new princess," Maleficent went on, stroking the raven that was sat on her shoulder. "What a happy day and what a grand celebration!"

"Thank you, Maleficent," said the king, uncertainly.

"Of course, I was rather surprised not to receive an invitation ..." Maleficent said, "However–"

"You weren't wanted!" burst out Merryweather and the other fairies clapped their hands over her mouth in horror.

"Not want–?" Maleficent looked shocked,

but quickly her features formed themselves into a cruel smirk and her eyes narrowed.

"Well, an oversight I am sure," she said, "I won't hold it against any of you."

"Really?" asked the Queen. "You … you're not angry?"

"Angry? Why, no," Maleficent's cruel smile widened. "And to prove there are no hard feelings, I would like to offer the little princess a gift myself!"

11

Everyone gasped in fear and the three good fairies gathered protectively in front of the crib.

"The princess surely will grow in grace and beauty," Maleficent said, "and will walk in peace and happiness, adored by all who know her. But, before the sun sets on her sixteenth birthday ... she will prick her finger on the spindle of a spinning wheel ... and DIE!" A crack of green lightning shot upwards from Maleficent's sceptre, marking the evil prophecy.

"No!" cried the fairies who looked at the innocent princess in despair.

"Seize her!" cried King Stefan, pointing at Maleficent. Twenty guards hurried towards the evil fairy, but they were blocked by a flash of green light from her sceptre.

"Fools!" cried Maleficent, "Do you

really think you can stop me?" She cackled
loudly. The sound echoed throughout the
castle and then the evil fairy disappeared
in a cloud of greenish-grey smoke,
leaving behind only a dark shadow on
the floor and her evil curse upon the
Princess Aurora.

A sad, quiet hush descended on the great
hall, as King Stefan and his Queen gathered
up the baby princess in their arms, tears

falling from their eyes. The three good fairies wiped their eyes and reached out to try and console the king and Queen.

"Is there some spell you can cast to undo this fateful curse?" asked the king, desperately. Flora, Fauna and Merryweather looked at each other in dejection.

"Maleficent's evil magic is too strong for us," said Flora, "but Merryweather still has her gift to give to the princess."

"Just do your best, dear," Fauna urged Merryweather, who stepped forwards to the crib. Determinedly, Merryweather raised her wand and took a deep breath.

"Sweet princess," the fairy said, "if, before your sixteenth birthday, this evil curse should strike, be it not in death, but only sleep you shall lie. In sweet repose you shall rest, until True Love's Kiss comes to break the spell."

Merryweather's spell was cast. The king and Queen were relieved that, should the princess prick her finger on a spinning wheel, she would only fall fast asleep. But still, the king could not bear to think of his beautiful daughter lying asleep for years and years, unable to live her life with joy and happiness.

"Every spinning wheel in the kingdom is to be burned!" the king ordered, and the guards rushed far and wide to obey his command.

Chapter Two

$\mathcal{T}$he three good fairies watched that night as the bonfire burned outside the castle. All the spinning wheels in the

kingdom had been found and burned, but they still weren't sure if the princess was safe from the evil curse.

"A bonfire won't stop Maleficent," said Merryweather grumpily, using her wand to light the candles in the castle bedroom.

Fauna thought for a moment. "Maybe we could reason with her?" she suggested.

"Reason? With Maleficent? Not a chance!" said Flora. She thought for a moment. "If only there were something we could do that she wouldn't be expecting! Something she couldn't know about."

Fauna thought hard. "Well, there is something Maleficent doesn't know about ...."

"What's that, dear?" asked Merryweather.

"Happiness," said Fauna. "Maleficent doesn't know anything about love, kindness or joy."

Suddenly, Flora whizzed up into the air, her wings fluttering excitedly. "I've got it!" she exclaimed. "Follow me!"

Flora turned herself, Fauna and Merryweather into tiny little fairies and they flew into a small teapot so they could talk in secret.

"Three peasant women," Flora said to the other two, "raising an orphan child in a little cottage in the woods. It's the last thing Maleficent would understand – a kind, selfless gesture!"

Fauna looked confused. "That is very nice of them, Flora," she said, "but who are these peasant women?"

Flora smiled and with a wave of her wand she changed Fauna's fairy gown into a plain peasant's dress. Fauna gasped when she caught sight of her reflection.

"Why, it's me! It's us!" she cried.

Flora nodded eagerly, changed her clothes and Merryweather's too.

"Exactly!" Flora said. "We shall disguise ourselves as peasant women and raise the Princess Aurora in a little cabin in the woods. No-one will know she is there, and it is the last thing that would arouse Maleficent's suspicions! She will be safe!"

"It's a brilliant idea!" exclaimed Merryweather. "And it will be so easy! With our magic–"

"Magic?" Flora interrupted. "Oh no! NO magic!"

"No magic?" replied Merryweather, frowning. "But how will we do anything?"

Flora grabbed Merryweather's wand, then Fauna's. "We will simply have to manage without. We can't do anything to arouse anyone's suspicions!"

Reluctantly, the other fairies agreed. They had to do everything they could to keep Princess Aurora safe and if that meant no magic, then no magic it would have to be.

The three good fairies flew out of the teapot and when Flora had restored them to their normal size, they eagerly flew to the king and Queen to explain their plan.

At first, the king and Queen were very sad at the thought of their little daughter being taken from them. But gradually, they realized it was the only way to keep her safe from Maleficent's evil. The fairies promised to bring her back to the castle as soon as the sun had set on Aurora's sixteenth birthday, for only then could they be sure that Maleficent's prophecy had failed.

That night, under the cover of darkness, the three good fairies smuggled the baby princess away into the woods, with King Stefan and his Queen watching sadly from the castle window. Deep, deep into the forest they went, until they could be sure no-one would ever find them, especially Maleficent and her evil cronies. They found a lovely, abandoned cottage in the heart of the woods.

Chapter Three

 M any sad and lonely years passed for the king and Queen. They knew Aurora was safe with the three good fairies, but they couldn't help but wish she was with them. As the princess's sixteenth birthday at last drew near, they began to hope the evil prophecy had failed.

Meanwhile, thunder and green lightning were raging on the Forbidden Mountain.

"It's incredible!" Maleficent raged,

surrounded by green fire and casting evil shadows on the walls. "It's been nearly sixteen years and not a sign of the princess! I told you to search the kingdom far and wide!" she screamed at one of her guards. "Why have you not found her yet?!"

"Apologies, your excellency!" the guard quivered with fear. "We have searched everywhere! Every house, every room, every cradle ...."

"Cradle?" Maleficent froze mid-stride. "Cradle? Did you hear that my precious?" she

stroked her pet raven. "All this time they've been looking for a BABY!"

Maleficent burst into peals of laughter, and the guards joined in foolishly, not understanding their mistake.

"IDIOTS!" Maleficent screamed and the guards cowered in the corner. "Do I have to do everything myself?"

Sparks of red-hot lightning shot out from her sceptre and her soldiers ran from the room squealing.

Maleficent sank down onto her black throne in despair, stroking her pet raven.

"My precious," she sighed, "you are my last hope. Spread your wings, fly far and wide. Any sign of the princess, anything suspicious, come to me immediately. Don't disappoint me ...."

The raven flew out of the castle window, and soared over the kingdom, determined to find the lost princess.

Deep in the forest, Princess Aurora had grown into a beautiful young woman. She had spent many happy years in the cottage with the three good fairies, who had raised her as their own child and named her Briar Rose. She had no idea of her true identity. Today was a very special day. It was finally Aurora's sixteenth birthday and although she did not know it, the three fairies were planning to take her back to the castle that evening. As soon as the sun set, it would mean Maleficent's evil prophecy had failed and Aurora would be free to finally live as a princess and marry Prince Phillip. The fairies were so excited. They planned to spend the day making a cake for Briar Rose and a beautiful dress fit for a princess.

"Rose! Briar Rose!" called Fauna. "Could you please go and pick some berries from the forest?"

Briar Rose, who had been reading in her room, came down the stairs. She was wearing her plain, grey peasant dress and her long hair was held back with a black hairband. Fauna smiled to herself happily. After tonight, Briar Rose would have all the beautiful ball gowns she could ever dream of!

"Berries?" said Briar Rose, smiling. "But I picked berries yesterday!"

"Um, well yes. I mean, we need more. Lots more!" said Fauna.

"Yes, lots more berries!" chimed in Merryweather. They had to get Briar Rose out of the cottage so they could plan the surprise birthday celebrations!

Briar Rose hid a smile. She could tell that Flora, Fauna and Merryweather were up to something, but she didn't want to ruin the surprise – whatever it was! She gathered together her shawl and her basket and kissed each of them in turn.

"Goodbye dear!"

"Take care!"

"And remember, don't talk to strangers!"

The three good fairies had always warned Briar Rose never to talk to anyone outside of the cottage. That way, they could be sure that no-one would grow suspicious of the beautiful young woman who lived in the woods.

Briar Rose waved goodbye and set off into the woods, humming gently to herself.

As soon as the door was shut, Flora clapped her hands.

"Right! We have a lot of work to do before Briar Rose gets back! Fauna, you bake the cake, I'll make the dress and Merryweather, you're in charge of cleaning up!"

Merryweather frowned. Why did she always get the least interesting jobs? She set off upstairs in a huff.

"I'll get the wands," she muttered.

"Wands?!" Flora stopped in the middle of the room. "No! No wands! We can't take any chances!"

"But Flora," Merryweather said, "How can we do all this without magic? Fauna has never made a cake before and you don't know the first thing about making dresses!"

"Well, we'll just have to do our best, won't we? After all, how hard can it be? Now, on second thoughts, stand on this stool, Merryweather. You can be the model for the dress." Flora started to rummage through her materials box.

Fauna gazed in bewilderment at the mountain of ingredients in front of her. Eggs, sugar, flour, milk … she had everything she needed, but no idea what to do with it all.

Determinedly, she rolled up her sleeves and turned to her recipe book.

"Mix flour, milk and eggs, with 2 tsps of salt," she murmured to herself. "Tsps?"

"Teaspoons, dear," said Merryweather, from underneath Flora's lengths of material.

"Oh yes! Teaspoons of course!" Fauna blushed and hastily grabbed some eggs, which she proceeded to fold into the mixture – whole.

Flora covered Merryweather in bright pink cloth and cut out a hole for the feet to go through. Merryweather examined the material in dismay.

"But I wanted it blue!" she cried.

"Now then," said Flora, "pink is a much better colour for a princess! Imagine how beautiful she's going to look tonight!"

The three good fairies got to work, determined to make this birthday surprise the best ever for their Briar Rose.

Elsewhere, in the forest, Briar Rose was singing happily as she wandered past the berry bushes. Her beautiful voice rang through the trees and caught the attention of the birds that were resting in their nests. Soon the whole forest was listening to the harmony. They all loved Briar Rose dearly, for they often joined her for her walks in the woods. She was so gentle and kind. She often told them her dreams and wishes, for she had no other friends to talk to.

But what they didn't know, was that the wind had carried Briar Rose's beautiful voice to another pair of ears.

The prince was taking his horse, Samson, for a run in the woods. They had been splashing through ponds, jumping hedges and racing, and were now about to turn back to the castle. Just as they were nearing the edge of the woods, the prince heard a wonderful sound. He pulled on Samson's

reigns and the horse stopped.

"Listen to that, Samson!" said the prince, in wonder. "It sounds like … singing!" The prince pulled his horse in the direction of the song. Stubbornly, Samson yanked his head in the direction of the castle. He was tired – and hungry!

"Oh, come on boy!" the prince leaned down to whisper in Samson's ear. "We'll just take a quick look!"

Samson shook his head.

"I'll give you an extra bucket of oats!"

Samson's eyes widened at this.

"And how about a few … carrots?" The prince smiled.

Samson gave in at the thought of his favourite treat and he and the prince sped off in search of the enchanting voice ringing through the trees.

Chapter Four

*B*riar Rose wandered through the forest, picking berries and talking to her animal friends.

"I wonder," she said softly, gazing at two little birds perched on the branch in front of her, "if each little bird has a special someone, surely there must be a special someone out there for me?" She sighed and walked over to the edge of the forest. There, in the distance, was King Stefan and his Queen's castle.

Little did Aurora know, this was to be her home from that night onwards.

Briar Rose sighed. "Why do they still treat me like a child?"

"Hoo? Hoo?" hooted the owl.

"Why, Flora, Fauna and Merryweather," she answered. "They never want me to meet anyone." Briar Rose took one last, lingering look at the castle in the distance, then turned back to the forest. Suddenly, she smiled at her friends.

"But you know what?" she said, her eyes sparkling. "I have met someone!"

The birds fluttered their wings in excitement. "Hoo? Hoo?" hooted the owl again.

"Why … a prince!" said Aurora. All the animals jumped up and down with happiness. A prince!

"He's tall, handsome and very romantic!

We walk together and talk together and share all of our dreams!" Briar Rose went on. "And then, when it gets dark, my prince takes me in his arms … and …."

The birds, squirrels and rabbits leaned forward eagerly.

"… I wake up." finished Briar Rose, as she sat back sadly. "Yes, it's only in my dreams."

The animals shook their heads in sorrow. They had so wanted their beautiful Briar

Rose to have found true love! If only there was something they could do to help! Just as they were about to give up, the owl noticed something in the bushes a little way off. He flew over to get a better look.

The owl rubbed his eyes in astonishment. There were clothes hanging from a branch in the trees! There was a hat, some trousers, a pair of boots and a cape – why, these were clothes fit for a prince. This gave the owl a brilliant idea ….

Little did the animals know, that these were the prince's clothes! Samson had been so excited at the thought of carrots that he ran headlong into a pond, tipping the prince right off and soaking him from head to foot! The prince had hung his clothes up to dry and was sitting in the sunshine daydreaming about the beautiful voice he had heard. He was so lost in his thoughts, he didn't notice the animals running off with all his clothes! Fortunately, Samson did notice and he whinnied loudly to get the prince's attention.

"What it is, boy?" Prince Phillip asked. He turned around just in time to see the owl flying off with his cape, the rabbits hopping away in his boots and the squirrels carrying his hat off.

"Hey! Hey, stop!" the prince cried chasing after them.

The owl was very proud of his idea. They would disguise themselves as a prince and Briar Rose would finally have someone to dance and sing with! Carefully, the owl placed the hat on his head – which was so big it nearly covered his eyes – and the birds draped the cape round his neck. The rabbits hopped into the boots to make it look as

though he was walking. Pleased with the finished results, the animals flew and hopped their prince disguise to Briar Rose.

Briar Rose was shaken out of her daydream by the sparrows next to her fluttering nervously.

"What is it?" she asked and looked around her. She tried not to laugh as she saw the owl and the rabbits dressed up as a prince walking towards her. How funny they looked!

Briar Rose didn't want to hurt their feelings, so she played along with the disguise.

"Why! It's my prince! He's finally here!" she cried and pretended to curtsey. "Will you dance with me?"

Wrapping the cape around her shoulders as if they were arms, Briar Rose began to dance with her 'prince'. The animals smiled at each other. The disguise was working!

"I know you, I walked with you once upon a dream …" Briar Rose sang, her voice trilling through the trees.

Prince Phillip, who had been running after his stolen clothes, stopped dead at the sight in front of him. There were his clothes, dancing with the most beautiful girl he had ever seen! And her voice – that was the wondrous sound he had been trying to find! He shook his head in disbelief and

stepped forward, determined to talk to this mysterious maiden.

"… once upon a dream …" Briar Rose continued to sing, dancing happily with her 'prince'. Suddenly, a voice joined in with hers!

"The way you did once …" sang Prince Phillip, "upon a dream!" He grasped Briar Rose's hands with his and continued the dance.

Briar Rose gasped and stepped back in shock.

"Oh, I'm sorry!" said Prince Phillip, quickly, "I didn't mean to frighten you!"

Briar Rose backed away from the handsome stranger. She had never met anyone in the forest before.

"Oh, please don't run!" the prince stepped towards her. "I just want to talk to you!"

"Talk? To me?" Briar Rose didn't know what to say. This boy was charming, handsome and he had such kind eyes … surely there could be no harm in talking to him? She couldn't help but smile at him.

"And anyway," Prince Phillip stepped forward and gently took her hand, "we've met before. You said so yourself!"

Briar Rose gazed into Phillip's warm brown eyes. "I did?" she asked.

"Yes. Once upon a dream ..." Prince Phillip started to dance with Briar Rose and soon the pair were waltzing under the twilight sky, little fireflies twinkling over the lake. Her animal friends looked on in happiness. They could tell that Briar Rose was finally falling in love.

"This has been a magical evening," Briar Rose said happily, resting her head on Phillip's shoulder. "I wish it didn't have to end."

Phillip placed his arms around her. "Me too," he whispered gently. They watched the sun start to lower in the sky and the evening shadows began to gather around them.

"What's your name?" Prince Phillip asked, realizing he had no idea who this beautiful girl was.

"My name? Why it's ..." Briar Rose hesitated. The fairies had warned her never to tell anyone her name! Should she tell him, without asking them first? Plus it was getting dark, they would be wondering where she was!

In a panic, Briar Rose broke away from Phillip's embrace.

"Oh no, I can't!" she cried, flustered.

"What?" said Phillip in alarm. "What's wrong?"

"Oh, I simply must go!" Briar Rose

gathered her basket and shawl and began to run away, towards the cottage.

"Wait!" cried the prince, "Stop! When shall I see you again?"

"Oh ..." Briar Rose gasped, "tonight! Later tonight! Come to the little cottage ... in the glen!" her voice trailed away as she ran off into the sunset.

Chapter Five

Unaware of what was happening in the woods between Briar Rose and the handsome stranger, the three good fairies had been hard at work on the birthday surprises.

Fauna wiped her brow and stood back to marvel at her cake. She frowned slightly.

The cake was a strange, whitish-yellow colour. The icing was dripping onto the table and the top three tiers were beginning to sag downwards. In fact, it looked as if the whole thing was about to collapse!

"It'll look much better once it's cooked!" Fauna assured Flora and Merryweather, who looked unconvinced.

Merryweather turned and examined the dress Fauna had made for Briar Rose. There were pink bows stuck at odd places all over it, the belt was tightly wound in the middle and the sleeves nearly reached the floor.

"It looks awful!" she exclaimed.

"That's because it's on you, dear," muttered Flora and she scrutinized the dress. "Maybe if I add some more bows …"

Merryweather shook her head in despair and the ruffles on the pink dress shook, making her look like a large, pink blancmange.

"Oh, it's all dreadful!" she cried.

The three fairies looked at the sagging, drippy cake, the disastrous pink dress and then at each other. Merryweather was right. This wasn't fit for Briar Rose's birthday celebration, let alone fit for a princess!

"That settles it," said Merryweather, jumping down from the stool. "I'm getting the wands."

Flora started to protest, but then closed her mouth. Even she couldn't deny that a little magic was exactly what they needed right now. But they had to be careful!

"Wait, Merryweather! Fauna! Close all the doors and windows! Block up every nook and cranny! We can't take any chances!"

All three of them darted around the cottage, blocking up mouse holes, drawing the blinds down over the windows and stuffing rags into the keyholes. Only then did they dare to bring the wands downstairs.

"Right!" said Flora, when they each had their wands in hand. "I'll do the dress! Fauna, you'll do the cake! And Merryweather … you're in charge of cleaning up."

Merryweather glared at Flora, who was already surrounded by long lengths of beautiful pink material, which was busy shaping itself into an exquisite gown, fit for a princess.

Sighing, Merryweather tapped her wand three times against the closet and immediately the broom, bucket and dustpan and brush busied themselves sweeping and polishing the room.

Fauna showed all her ingredients the recipe book and within minutes a large, delicious-looking cake was beginning to form itself! There were six tiers covered with delicate pink icing, little white gemdrops and raspberry swirls.

Satisfied that the household utensils were doing their job, Merryweather sat back and admired the cake – and the dress. The dress had a long, swirling skirt, gorgeous satin sleeves and it was ... pink. Merryweather frowned. She hated pink. She wanted the dress to be blue, just like her own. Briar Rose would look so much prettier in blue ....

Pretending to supervise the sweeping broom, Merryweather waited till Flora's back was turned and then flicked her wand towards the dress.

"Make it blue!" she commanded and instantly the dress transformed into a shimmering, ocean blue.

Flora turned back to the dress and gasped in horror. She glared at Merryweather, who was innocently watching the cloths clean the windows, and flicked her own wand.

"Make it pink!" Flora commanded. The dress turned back to bright pink.

Merryweather moved over to the stairs and pretended to polish the banister.

"Make it blue!" she flicked her wand again.

"Make it pink!" cried Flora.

"Make it blue!"

"Pink!"

"Blue!"

Flora and Merryweather were so caught up in their silly argument, they didn't realize that the flashes of pink and blue had caught someone – or something's – attention ….

Maleficent's raven had been soaring over the forest. He had not caught even a glimpse of anything suspicious and was quivering with fear at the thought of Maleficent's wrath when she discovered that he, too, had failed her.

Just as he was about to turn and fly back to the castle, he noticed something peculiar out the corner of his eye. In the distance, amongst the thickest trees in the wood, a sudden flash of pink appeared. He floated in the air, watching with interest. Then, a spark of blue flashed through the trees. Then pink again! Curious, the raven flew towards these

mysterious lights. He followed the colourful flashes, down into the trees, until the woodcutter's cottage in the glen appeared in front of him. The pink and blue sparks were coming from the chimney. In their haste, the fairies had forgotten to block it up! The raven landed on the windowsill, and peered through the window ....

"Pink!"

"BLUE!"

With this last 'blue', Merryweather accidentally aimed her wand at Flora,

turning her dress blue. Merryweather giggled. Flora quivered with rage and aimed her wand at Merryweather. "Pink!" The two fairies chased each other all over the house, pink and blue flashing everywhere! Finally, their two wands hit the beautiful dress at the same time, leaving it an ugly mish-mash of blue and pink.

"Oh! Now looked what you've done! Enough of this nonsense! Let's tidy all of this up – Briar Rose will be back any minute!" The three fairies hurried to get everything ready.

Just at that moment they heard Briar Rose's sweet voice approaching the door.

"Hide!" whispered Flora and they all flitted over to conceal themselves behind the couch.

Just then, the door opened and Briar Rose found herself standing in a quiet, dark cottage. Puzzled, she took off her shawl and set her basket down on the floor.

"Hello?" she called. "Is there anyone…oh!"

She caught sight of the wonderful ball gown in the centre of the room.

"Surprise!" cried the three fairies, running out from behind the couch and gathering Briar Rose in a big hug.

"Happy Birthday!" added Fauna, nodding towards the cake.

"Oh my goodness!" exclaimed Briar Rose, hugging each fairy in turn. "You lovely dears! This is so wonderful!" She ran over to examine the dress more closely.

"This is the happiest day of my life!" She turned back to Flora, Fauna and Merryweather, her eyes shining. The three fairies beamed. This is exactly what they had hoped for – a special day for their special Briar Rose.

"Oh, just wait till you meet him!" Briar

Rose went on. The three fairies frowned.

"Him? Who? Did you meet someone, dear?" the fairies asked all at once.

Briar Rose nodded her head.

"W-where?" stammered Fauna.

"Why, once upon a dream!" Briar Rose laughed and began to dance round the room with Fauna.

"Why, it looks like she's … she's …" Flora paused.

"… in love," finished Merryweather.

Flora clapped her hands over her mouth.

"Oh no!" she said, through her fingers. "This is terrible!"

"Terrible?" Briar Rose paused in her dancing and looked at Flora with a puzzled smile. "It's wonderful! I can't wait to see him again! He's tall, handsome …" she trailed off as she saw the solemn look on the three faces in front of her.

"What on earth's the matter?" Briar Rose asked, anxiously.

"I'm sorry my dear. But you can never see that young man again." Flora said, sadly.

"But, what … what do you mean?" Briar Rose paled slightly. "He's coming here tonight! He's coming to meet you all!"

Flora shook her head.

"But, my dear, you won't be here tonight," she said, gently. "It's time to tell you the truth."

The fairies walked up to Briar Rose and took her hands in theirs.

"My dear, you are a princess. Princess Aurora."

Briar Rose's eyes widened in shock.

"Today you are sixteen and we can take you back to the castle tonight to reunite you with your true mother and father. That is the reason you can never see your young man again.

That … and because you are betrothed."

"But … but …" Aurora's eyes filled with tears and her lip began to wobble.

"To a prince! Prince Phillip!" Fauna added, hopefully.

"No!" Briar Rose tore her hands away and covered her face. "No!" she burst into tears and ran from the room.

The three good fairies stood in the middle of the cottage, gazing sadly at the beautiful gown and cake they had made for this day.

"We thought she'd be so happy," said Fauna, wiping her eyes on her dress.

Meanwhile, Maleficent's raven, who had heard everything, flew as fast as he could back to the Forbidden Mountain. He couldn't wait to tell Maleficent that he had found Princess Aurora!

Chapter Six

King Stefan gazed out of a window in his castle, desperate for a glimpse of his daughter for the first time in sixteen years.

"There's still half an hour till sunset …" he said to King Hubert, who clapped him on the back.

"It's all in the past!" King Hubert said, cheerfully. "Nothing's going to happen in the next half an hour! Your princess will be here any moment, the kingdom will celebrate and

my Phillip and she will be together!" He raised a glass to toast his words.

"I hope you're right, Hubert," muttered King Stefan, worriedly. He would not be able to relax until the sun had set. Until it had, there was still the chance that Maleficent's evil prophecy could come true.

King Hubert came to the window. "Why, here's my Phillip now!"

Prince Phillip had just raced through the

gates of the castle on Samson. He couldn't wait to tell his father about the beautiful girl he had met that afternoon.

The king went down to meet his son in the courtyard.

"Father!" cried Prince Phillip as soon as he saw King Hubert. "I have the most wonderful news!"

King Hubert wasn't listening. He was too busy looking at his son's clothes.

"What's this?" he said in dismay. "You'd better tidy yourself up if you're going to meet your future bride!"

"But I have met her, Father!" said the prince, swooping his father up in an embrace.

"You have? But … where?" King Hubert strained to look over Phillip's shoulder, hoping to catch a glimpse of Princess Aurora.

"Once upon a dream …" Prince Phillip laughed, dancing around with his father.

"What? What's this nonsense?" King Hubert pulled away from his son and straightened his clothes. "Stop all this, Phillip, and come inside."

"It's not nonsense, Father. I really did meet her! I'm going to her cottage tonight to ask her to marry me!"

"Cottage? Princesses don't live in cottages!" King Hubert spluttered, confused.

"She isn't a princess, Father!" Phillip laughed. "She's a peasant girl I met in the woods!"

"Peasant girl ... PEASANT GIRL?" King Hubert went bright red with anger. "Phillip, you are a prince and you are to marry a princess! You can't do this to me!"

The prince backed away from his father and remounted his horse. "There's nothing you can say, Father. I met the girl I love and I am going to find her right now. Goodbye, Father!"

King Hubert watched in despair as his son rode back out through the castle gates. How was he ever going to tell King Stefan that his son would rather marry a peasant girl than Princess Aurora?

As Prince Phillip raced to the cottage in the woods, the three good fairies and Princess Aurora arrived in secret at the castle. The fairies took Aurora to the tower, to prepare her for the grand reunion that night. Aurora sat down sadly at the dressing table. Solemnly, the fairies put their three wands together in the air.

"One last gift, child. For your life as a princess," said Flora.

A beautiful, golden crown appeared in the

air and Flora gently set it upon Aurora's head. Aurora gazed at herself in the mirror and at the crown upon her head. She looked exactly like a princess should, yet all she could think of was the young man she had met in the woods and how they would never be together.

"Let's give her a few moments alone," suggested Merryweather and they walked quietly out of the room, closing the door softly behind them.

Aurora sobbed at the unfairness of it all. Why, on the day she had finally met her true love, was she suddenly whisked away from him and all that she knew?

Aurora was crying so much, she didn't notice that the candles in the room had dimmed and were slowly going out one-by-one, leaving her in the gloom. A dark, shifting shadow appeared by the fireplace and a green glow seemed to be coming from it.

Aurora looked up and blinked away her tears. The green glow grew brighter and she found herself unable to look away from it. The room grew darker still, until all the princess could see was the mysterious, seductive light. Slowly, as if she were hypnotized, she got up from her chair and walked towards it. The light seemed to hover

in the air, then it began to move away, leading Aurora to the fireplace. It stopped, then, as if by magic, a secret doorway appeared.

In a trance, Aurora followed the green glow through the doorway and began to climb a long, dark staircase, which led up to the highest tower in the castle.

The three good fairies, unaware of what was happening, were sitting in the next room, their heads resting glumly on their hands.

"Whatever shall we do?" murmured Fauna. "She is so sad."

"Maybe, when she meets Prince Phillip–" began Merryweather, but Flora cut her off.

"Ssssshhh!" Flora hissed, her head turned in the direction of Aurora's room. She thought she heard something, something … strange. The three fairies listened carefully. Just when Flora thought she must have been mistaken, they heard the sound again. A low, haunting, murmuring sound, which almost sounded like ... 'Au-ro-ra'.

Flora gasped in horror.

"Maleficent!" she cried, and the three fairies ran into Aurora's room, just in time to see the princess follow the green light through the secret passage.

"No!" shouted Merryweather and the fairies chased after Aurora – but the door vanished!

"Stand back!" ordered Flora and with a dart of her wand she created another doorway. The fairies flew as fast as they could up the staircase.

The princess had reached the top of the stairs, totally entranced by the mysterious green glow. It led her into a small room and she obediently followed. Suddenly the green light flashed brightly, and there, in the middle of the room appeared … a spinning wheel. Aurora moved nearer. The green glow came to rest on the top of the sharp, pointed spindle and a low voice seemed to surround the princess.

"Touch the spindle … touch it!" the voice said.

Aurora stretched out her hand and delicately placed her finger on the sharp spindle. There was a crack of lightning and Maleficent appeared in the room, laughing wickedly.

The three good fairies burst into the room – but they were too late.

"Fools!" cried Maleficent triumphantly. "Did you really think you could deceive me?"

The fairies cowered in terror.

"Here's your precious princess!" cried Maleficent and with a wave of her black coat she revealed the Princess Aurora, lying in a crumpled heap on the floor.

The three good fairies cried out in despair and Maleficent disappeared in a cloud of green smoke, her cruel laughter echoing all around them.

Chapter Seven

King Hubert approached King Stefan's throne nervously. However was he going to tell him Prince Phillip had run off to the woods to propose to a peasant girl, on the very evening the princess was due to finally return?

He opened his mouth to speak, but just then, a loud fanfare sounded and fireworks began to explode in the sky. It was sunset!

"Sunset!" cried King Stefan and his

Queen. "Where is Aurora?" They hugged each other happily and gazed at the main doors of the castle.

But, up in the highest tower, Flora, Fauna and Merryweather were wiping away their silent tears as they gazed down on the happy scene below them. Princess Aurora lay on a small bed in the room behind them, lost in a deep, deep sleep.

"Poor King Stefan and the Queen," sobbed Fauna, "they will be heartbroken. However are we going to tell them?"

Flora patted her on the back, wiping away her own tears. She thought for a moment.

"We won't tell them." Flora said, decisively.

"But Flora–" Merryweather began, but Flora raised her hand to silence her.

"We'll put them all to sleep," Flora

announced. "The whole kingdom. They can all join Aurora in her slumber, until we can find True Love's Kiss to wake her. Then, they can all wake up together and it will be as if no time has passed at all."

The fairies nodded at each other. It seemed like the only way. With a heavy heart, Merryweather used her wand to make herself as small as a butterfly and flew out of the castle window, down to the crowds below.

She flew over guards, butlers, servants and cooks, who all fell to the ground in a deep slumber as the magic sleeping dust from Merryweather's wand floated gently down to touch their eyelids. She dimmed all the candles in the castle one-by-one, to make the everlasting sleep as peaceful as possible for everyone.

Flora flew down to join her and sprinkled her magic sleeping dust over King Stefan, the Queen and King Hubert.

King Hubert was still trying to explain to King Stefan about Prince Phillip, but he was already starting to yawn so much he could barely get the words out.

"So you see ... Stefan," King Hubert yawned to an already half-asleep King Stefan, "if Phillip wants to marry a peasant girl ... there really isn't anything I can do ..." his eyelids drooped.

Flora stopped dead. Peasant girl?

Quickly, she flew back to King Hubert and whispered right in his ear.

"Peasant girl? What peasant girl?" she hissed eagerly.

King Hubert was struggling to keep his eyes open.

"Oh, just some … peasant girl …" he mumbled as his eyes began to close.

"But who?" Flora insisted, yanking his eyelids open with her wand. "Where did he meet her?"

"Once upon … a dream …" King Hubert murmured and finally fell fast asleep.

Once upon a dream! Flora's eyes went as wide as saucers. That was just what Aurora said, back in the cottage … the boy she had met in the woods that afternoon was really Prince Phillip! That meant that he was her true love and therefore he could break the spell!

Flora shot back to Fauna and Merryweather as fast as her wings could carry her. They had to get back to the cottage in the woods and find Prince Phillip!

At that very moment, Prince Phillip was approaching the cottage. He straightened his hat, took a deep breath and knocked firmly on the door.

"Come in," a quiet, female voice said from within.

Prince Phillip opened the door and was surprised to find the cottage in darkness. He squinted through the gloom. Just as he opened his mouth to speak, a voice came from the corner of the room.

"NOW!"

Prince Phillip felt a rough, heavy sack being forced over his head and his hands tied painfully behind his back. It was Maleficent and her guards! The raven knew Aurora had arranged to meet him at the cottage that night and had told Maleficent everything. She wasn't going to risk the princess being awoken by True Love's Kiss and planned to keep him tied up in her castle on the Forbidden Mountain.

She smirked at the young man who was

desperately struggling against the guards.

"Why, look at this! I came expecting to capture some peasant boy and I manage to catch a prince! Take him to the dungeon!" she ordered and the guards raced out of the cottage, dragging poor Prince Phillip behind them.

As Maleficent and her evil cronies disappeared into the night, the three good fairies were flying as fast as they could to the cottage. When they reached the front door, they gripped each other's hands.

"Oh, I hope we're not too late!" whispered Fauna.

Cautiously, they pushed the door open. Lighting their wands against the darkness, they examined the cottage.

"He isn't here ..." whispered Merryweather.

Just then, Flora let out a cry of dismay and pointed at something lying on the ground. It was Prince Phillip's hat.

"We're too late," Flora said, desperately. "Maleficent has taken him to the Forbidden Mountain!"

"What shall we do?" moaned Fauna, wringing her hands. The three fairies looked at each other.

"There's only one thing we can do." Flora said firmly. They had to rescue Prince Phillip from Maleficent's castle – it was their only chance of ever waking Princess Aurora from her eternal sleep. Merryweather and Fauna nodded and bravely the three good fairies set off for the Forbidden Mountain.

Chapter Eight

*T*he rain was pounding down and the sky was black and purple as the three good fairies approached Maleficent's mountain home. Making themselves as small as sparrows, the fairies hid behind a stone and peered over at the monstrous guard who was marching in front of the door. Flora waited until his back was turned and hissed – "Now!"

As quick as a flash, the fairies darted down and flew through a crack in the wall.

Relieved they hadn't been spotted, they stopped to rest. Just then, they heard loud, chanting coming from a great hall down below them. Fearfully, they flew to see what was happening.

All of Maleficent's cronies were dancing and singing around an enormous green bonfire, celebrating the capture of Prince Phillip, the princess's true love.

Maleficent watched the festivities, a nasty smile playing on her lips.

"What a pity Prince Phillip can't be here to enjoy the celebrations," she smirked. "Let's go down to the dungeon and cheer him up!"

Maleficent walked slowly down to the deepest, darkest room in her castle and the three good fairies followed, being sure to stay hidden.

She unlocked the door and stepped

inside. Prince Phillip narrowed his eyes against the sudden light and then scowled at the sinister figure in front of him. Maleficent chuckled cruelly and approached the prince, who was tied to the castle wall with heavy chains.

She held up her sceptre and the ball on the top of it began to glow green.

"I've got something to show you, handsome prince ..." Maleficent sneered

and gradually a picture began to form in the air in front of them.

Prince Phillip's eyes widened. It was the girl from the forest! But she was wearing a crown ...

"That's right, prince," Maleficent said, the picture of Aurora swirling in the air in front of them. "Your peasant girl, your true love, is really your betrothed – Princess Aurora!"

"Alas," Maleficent went on, as the prince struggled to understand, "she is in the grip of everlasting sleep, a spell that can only be broken by True Love's Kiss. What a shame you are locked up in here …."

The prince struggled against his chains, but it was no use. Maleficent laughed and turned to leave the room, leaving the vision of the beautiful sleeping princess hanging in the air to torture him.

The three good fairies, who had been watching through the keyhole, waited till they heard Maleficent walk the steep steps up to her tower before flying down to set the prince free.

"Sssh! No time to explain!" whispered Flora as she removed Prince Phillip's gag and he opened his mouth to speak. With a flash from her wand she released the chains that were binding his wrists and feet.

Merryweather stepped back, swirled her wand in the air and suddenly a majestic shield and a bright, large sword appeared in Prince Phillip's hands.

"This is the Shield of Virtue and the mighty Sword of Truth," Merryweather told the prince. "Use them well and they will triumph over evil."

The prince gripped the weapons tightly

and followed the fairies out of the dungeon.

"This way!" whispered Fauna and they began to lead Prince Phillip up the stairs to the castle doors. Just as they reached the top, there was a loud SQUAWK! It was Maleficent's raven. They had been spotted!

The raven was flying speedily to warn Maleficent. Merryweather chased it angrily.

"Why, you puffed-up pigeon!" she cried and a stream of sparks came whizzing from her wand, hitting the raven straight in the chest.

With a final squawk, the raven froze on the wall outside Maleficent's tower. Merryweather had turned him to stone! With a satisfied nod, she turned to rejoin her friends and the prince.

Hearing a commotion, Maleficent opened the door of her tower to see what was happening. Spotting her raven sitting on the wall, she asked him what was going on. When he didn't answer, Maleficent frowned and peered at him.

"No!" she let out a cry of rage as she realized her beloved pet had been turned to stone. "NO!"

Maleficent thrust her sceptre in the air and a fork of hot, white lightning lit up the sky and the mountain. She cast her eyes around and they landed on the prince, who was racing through the gates on his horse with the three good fairies flying closely behind him.

Gritting her teeth with rage, Maleficent sent bolts of lightning shooting down to block the prince's path. Samson reared up in fear, but Prince Phillip steered him round the flames and they continued their race to the castle and the princess.

"Try getting through this, prince!" Maleficent screeched and directed her sceptre towards the castle. Suddenly, a thick, twisting forest of thorns surrounded the castle, blocking Phillip's path. Maleficent cackled wickedly.

The thorns were sharp like knives and the vines were like black snakes wrapped round each other tightly.

"The sword, Phillip!" cried Flora. The prince grasped his weapon, raising it high

in the air. He brought it down hard, cutting through the nasty, twisted forest. Chopping and cutting, the prince and his horse struggled bravely through the thorns, which ripped and clawed at his clothes. Just as he was beginning to lose hope, the prince caught sight of something through the black branches. It was the white stone of the castle! With new strength, the prince swiped his Sword of Truth through the air and, with the help of the fairies' magic wands, the last of the evil spikes fell to the ground.

Maleficent watched in disbelief.

"No!" she exclaimed. "It cannot be!"

In a storm of fury, Maleficent rose into the air and flew as quick as lightning towards the prince. Landing in front of him, she bared her teeth in a grimace of rage.

"Now you deal with me!" she spat and the prince watched in horror as she began to grow bigger and bigger, rising into the air in a cloud of purple and green smoke.

The three fairies looked on in dread as Maleficent towered over the prince. Her long, white face contorted into an evil snout and horrible black wings appeared on her back. A long, snaking tail sprouted from behind her and she hissed at the prince with a purple, forked tongue.

Maleficent had transformed herself into a fire-breathing dragon!

Desperately, the prince used his shield to defend himself from the flames shooting

from the dragon's mouth. Again and again she spewed evil fire from her belly, until the prince's shield was finally reduced to cinders.

The fairies gasped.

Dodging the flames, Prince Phillip scrambled to his feet and raced back into the thorns, trying to avoid the fire. He ran through the forest with the huge dragon looming behind him, until he came to the edge of the cliff. Narrowly avoiding the drop, Prince Phillip turned to face Maleficent, who hissed at him with her forked tongue.

"So much for true love!" she shrieked and her dragon's belly expanded as she took one final breath, ready to engulf the prince in fire one last time.

Prince Phillip gripped his sword and Merryweather cast her wand over it.

"Sword of Truth, fly swift and true!" she said and the prince flung it towards the dragon with all his might. It shot through the air and the long blade plunged into Maleficent's heart. Her dreadful scream echoed far and wide as she shrivelled and she sank to the ground engulfed in purple smoke. Soon, all that was left of Maleficent was the smouldering cinders of her black cloak.

The three fairies hugged each other and the prince with joy. Without a moment to lose, they made their way to the tower – and the sleeping beauty.

"Here she is," smiled Flora as they entered the chamber where Princess Aurora lay. The fairies stood back as Prince Phillip knelt down by her bed. She looked so peaceful, her golden hair spread out over the satin pillows. The prince leaned forward and kissed her gently on the lips.

For a moment, nothing happened. Then, Aurora's eyelids started to flutter.

"It's working!" squealed Fauna.

Slowly, the princess's eyes opened and Aurora looked on the face of her true love – Prince Phillip.

"It's you!" she exclaimed, and a smile spread across her face. The prince embraced his princess and the three good fairies wept with joy. The spell had been broken!

Downstairs, in the great hall, everyone else began to wake up. People staggered to their feet, looking dazed and confused. Guards glanced around guiltily, worried that they had been caught sleeping when on duty.

King Stefan rubbed his eyes and looked around him blearily.

"Ah, sorry Hubert," he mumbled to the sleepy king sitting next to him, "I must have dozed off for a minute! What were you saying? Something about a peasant girl?"

"Oh!" said King Hubert, blinking the sleep out of his eyes. "Well, it's like this, Stefan. My Phillip–"

He was cut short by a tremendous fanfare, which rang through the hall. King Stefan and his Queen jumped to their feet hopefully.

"Their Royal Highnesses," cried a court announcer, "Princess Aurora and Prince Phillip!"

The crowd gasped with delight as Aurora and Phillip began to walk down the grand staircase. Aurora was beaming with joy and the

beautiful gown the fairies had made for her
twinkled and shimmered. Her shining crown
sat on her golden hair.

Aurora ran to embrace her parents, who
embraced their daughter tightly. After all
these years, their princess was back where
she belonged, safe and sound.

Aurora turned back to smile at Prince
Phillip, who bowed to her parents. King
Hubert shook his head in confusion.

"But ... but ..." he stammered, not
able to believe his eyes. Here was his son,

not with a peasant girl, but with the princess! Shrugging his shoulders, he simply sat back and watched happily as Princess Aurora and Prince Phillip began to waltz round the castle hall.

Up on a balcony, the three good fairies gazed at their Princess Aurora through happy tears.

"Oh," sighed Flora, "I just love happy endings!"

The End